The whisper of a fairy
The magic of its word
Will help those in the forest
Whenever it is heard

And when there is danger
Wherever there is need
A fairy's care and help
Will be there indeed

a min@dition book
published by Penguin Young Readers Group

Text copyright © 2008 by Simone Lindner
Illustrations copyright © 2008 by Christa Unzner
Original title: Feuerelfe Runya
English text translation by Kathryn Bishop
Coproduction with Michael Neugebauer Publishing Ltd., Hong Kong.
Licensed by Margarete Steiff GmbH, Giengen, Germany
Rights arranged with "minedition" Rights and Licensing AG, Zurich, Switzerland.

Published simultaneously in Canada.
Manufactured in Hong Kong by Wide World Ltd.
Typesetting in Frutiger, by Adrian Frutiger.
Color separation by Fotoriproduzione Grafiche, Verona, Italy.

Library of Congress Cataloging-in-Publication Data available upon request.

ISBN 978-0-698-40071-9
10 9 8 7 6 5 4 3 2 1
First Impression

For more information please visit our website: www.minedition.com

Also published in this series:

Aelin, the Water Fairy
Amar, the Earth Fairy
Tara, the Air Fairy

Runya, the Fire Fairy

by Simone Lindner
Illustrated by Christa Unzner
Translated by Kathryn Bishop

minedition

Runya, the little Fire Fairy, hopped from
one sun-baked stone to another.

"Catch me if you can!"
Runya called to her shadow,
which skipped and jumped just as she did.
But the higher the sun rose in the sky,
the smaller the shadow became.
By noontime Runya could only see
a small dark circle around her feet.

Runya stretched, and she shook her flaming-red hair.
Her delicate fairy wings made a soft whirring sound.
A warm current carried her higher and higher.
Like a bird, the Fire Fairy floated past the cliffs,
did three somersaults in the air, and looked
down at the forest below.
The trees stood so calmly in the midday sun.
But Runya noticed a thin column of smoke
rising from a clearing in the forest,
and the smell of fire filled her nose.

Runya flew down, and seconds later stood beside a dried out tree stump where small, orange flames were already crackling.
"This can't be true," said Runya.
She stamped her foot furiously on the dry and dusty forest soil.
"What silly person left glass here in the forest?"
The thick pieces of broken glass had acted like a magnifying glass, causing the dry moss to burn.

The whole forest would be in danger when the strong afternoon wind came and spread the flames!
"I have to do something.
First the animals must be warned, and then I'll try to put out the fire," thought Runya.
There wasn't a moment to spare!

She lifted off, and with her red hair, Runya looked
like a ball of fire streaking through the forest.
"FIRE! There's a fire! You must all get to safety! FIRE!"
cried Runya as she flew from tree to tree. The quiet forest
suddenly became loud and frantic.

Birds twittered wildly.
The deer ran in every direction.
Lizards and snakes crept from their
hiding places.
A squirrel with orange-brown fur scurried
toward the Fire Fairy.

"Runya! What is it?" asked the squirrel.
"Oh, Pilin, am I glad to see you!" said Runya
as she hugged her friend. "We have to put
out the fire before it spreads!"

"Hey! What's going on up there?"
Runya and Pilin heard a squeaky voice from below.
The head of a mouse popped out from a hole next to a
burning stump.
"My children and I are trying to take a nap,"
she said.

Runya stared at the little mouse.
"What? Your little ones are still down
there? You have to get
them out now!" Runya shouted.
"There's a fire!"

The mother mouse disappeared instantly underground and
brought out one baby mouse after another.

Pilin carried them quickly to a clearing a safe distance away. "One, two, three, four, five… all here!" said the relieved mother as she sat with her children, trying to catch her breath.

"How am I going to put out the fire before it spreads?" wondered Runya. "The brook is too far away. There's nothing here but dirt, sand, and rocks. I don't even have a bucket. Think Runya, think!" She closed her eyes, breathed deeply three times, and whispered a chant from the world of magical beings.

Ni nalla tulu!
I call for help!

Heart of a fairy, brave and true
Show me now what I must do
Time is short there is no doubt
Fire and flames must be put out!

"That's it!" she said suddenly. "I can use the sand and dirt."
Runya made a bag for the sand out of leaves. Then she used
her scarf to protect her mouth and nose from the smoke.
She took off carrying the heavy load.
The little fairy emptied the sand directly over the crackling
flames. The first flames went out.

"It works!" cheered Runya. "But I need more."
Back and forth she flew carrying the sand and spreading it
over the fire.
Her arms were tired but
she didn't stop until
the last flames were out.

"You did it, Runya!" shouted Pilin. "You did it!"
He put the worn-out little fairy on his back
and carried her to the others.
The little mouse children sang, "The fire's out! Fire's out!
          Bad, bad fire's out!"

But Runya didn't want to hear that. After all, fire was
her element.
"Fire isn't always bad!" she said to the mouse children.
"Why don't you come and visit me tonight,
and I'll show you how important and
beautiful fire can be."

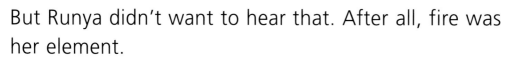

As the sun set, Pilin and the little mouse family arrived at Runya's home. Mother Mouse cried tears of joy as she thanked Runya again for rescuing them.

Runya had prepared a delicious meal. When they were finished with dinner, she placed a large pine cone in the glowing embers of the fire she had made, and gave her guests the roasted seeds. Runya laughed as the little mice rubbed their tummies, full at last.

"You see, without fire, the world wouldn't be nearly as nice!"

"We can cook with fire. And it gives us light and warmth.
But we must always be careful and keep a close eye on a fire."

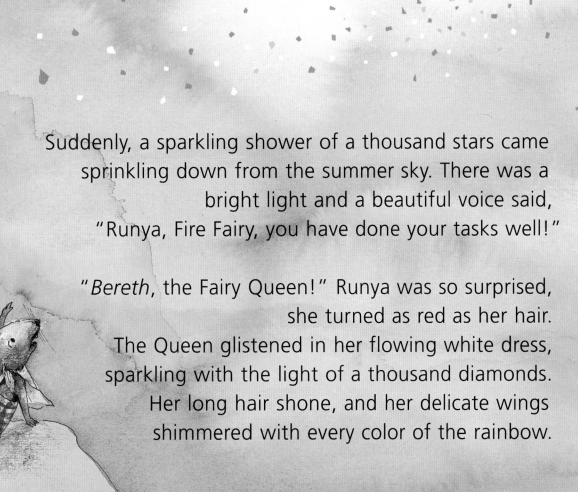

Suddenly, a sparkling shower of a thousand stars came
sprinkling down from the summer sky. There was a
bright light and a beautiful voice said,
"Runya, Fire Fairy, you have done your tasks well!"

"*Bereth*, the Fairy Queen!" Runya was so surprised,
she turned as red as her hair.
The Queen glistened in her flowing white dress,
sparkling with the light of a thousand diamonds.
Her long hair shone, and her delicate wings
shimmered with every color of the rainbow.

"Runya, you are a very
special Fire Fairy.
For a long time you have cared
for the plants and animals, for the
rocks and fire.
You have done this well.
I would like to send you into the world of
human children. Are you ready to go?"

Runya's face lit up and she nodded.
"Yes, I'm ready!" she said.

The Queen opened the petals of a red poppy
and took out a little ring made of gold.
"Runya, Fire Fairy, I hereby present to you the
magic ring of your element, fire."

"The ring will serve you in the human world.
It will help you exchange secret messages, and it will seal
your friendships. When it is placed on the ground,
it will create a large circle, and only those who enter it
will be able to see you, to speak and dance with you.

From now on you are to be a friend
and protector of a human child.
That child is reading this story and
is waiting for you."

Runya beamed and placed the ring
on her finger.

Then the shining light disappeared as suddenly as it had come.
For Runya, the Fire Fairy, a new adventure was about to begin…

Could her adventure be with *you?*

Which of the elements suits you best?

WATER and *Aelin*

1. imaginative
2. bubbly
3. creative
4. pure
5. lakes, rivers
6. sea, ocean
7. waves
8. waterfalls
9. raindrops, snowflakes
10. ice crystals
11. slide, float
12. swim

FIRE and *Runya*

1. fiery
2. warm-hearted
3. explosive
4. enthusiastic
5. full of energy
6. gives warmth
7. brings light in the darkness
8. sparkling
9. crackle
10. sun
11. fire light
12. firesides

EARTH and *Amar* ○

1. rascal
2. steadfast
3. healing abilities
4. good-natured
5. rocks and stones
6. mountains and valley
7. forests and meadows
8. earth, trees, and roots
9. plants and flowers
10. digging
11. playing in the sand
12. all 4 seasons

Air and *Tara* ◇

1. happy
2. playful
3. quick-tempered
4. wind
5. storm
6. sky
7. clouds
8. flying with birds
9. soaring, floating
10. feeling free as a breeze
11. feeling light as a feather
12. pinwheels and kites

When you have finished the book and have discovered the wonders of the fairy, open this letter. It was written especially for you!